HOTEL
FLAMINGO
FABULOUS FEAST

ALEX MILWAY

Piccadilly
PRESS

First published in Great Britain in 2020 by
PICCADILLY PRESS
80–81 Wimpole St, London W1G 9RE
www.piccadillypress.co.uk

A CIP catalogue record for this book is available from the British Library.

ISBN: 978-1-84812-839-2
also available as an ebook

1

Printed and bound in Poland

Piccadilly Press is an imprint of Bonnier Books UK
www.bonnierbooks.co.uk

For Cecily

CAN YOU
FIND ME
IN THE STORY?

Port Whisker

Sea Dog
Pirate Tours

Zoozoo Theme Park

Tusks Cinema

Le Chat Shopping Mall

Dukduk Bowling

The Boulevard
Sports Arena

ANIMAL BOULEVARD

Hotel Flamingo

Lookout
Point

Sandy Dunes

Savannah Beach

Fort Rhino

1

The Guest from Above

The snow was melting after a long, quiet winter, and the staff of Hotel Flamingo were determined to enjoy what little remained. There was always time for one last snowball fight.

'Duck!' yelled T. Bear.

'Where?' cried Anna, as a fresh ball of slushy ice knocked her hat off.

She slammed her fist into her palm.

'This means war!' she grumbled.

But before the battle could commence, Anna heard a crash and a clunk from the roof of the hotel.

'Miss Anna!' roared T. Bear, pointing upwards. 'DUCK!'

'I'm not falling for that again!' said Anna.

At that moment a bewildered and slightly frosty bird fell from the sky and crashed into the pavement, knocking Anna off her feet. T. Bear rushed over to help.

'Miss Anna!' he growled.

'Ouch!' said Anna.

'Sorry, ma'am,' said the bird, ruffling his feathers. He pulled his flight goggles up on to his head and helped Anna off the ground.

'It's OK,' she said, rubbing her arm.
'But you're no duck!'

'You're darn right,' he said. 'I'm a
pigeon. The name's Alfonso Fastbeak –'

The pigeon looked suddenly dizzy.

'– and I think I need to lie down.'

•

Alfonso was resting in a chair in the
lobby, enjoying a hot cocoa. All the staff
of Hotel Flamingo were huddled around
him, listening to his tales of derring-do.

'It was a triple loop with two forward
rolls,' he said, taking a sip of his drink.
'Followed by my signature move – the
Impossible Twisting Backflip!'

'Wow!' said Lemmy in awe.

'I know,' said Alfonso. 'I thought I had
time to complete the routine. I managed

the loops, but the backflip was a step too far and I ended up clanging into your roof.'

'Amazing,' said Eva. 'And you survived all that?'

'Sure was a close shave, ma'am,' said Alfonso.

'But why did you do it?' asked Anna. 'It sounds terrifying.'

'Miss, I am a stunt pigeon,' said Alfonso. 'It's what I do – or rather, it's what I did.'

He pulled out a poster from his pocket and handed it to Anna. It showed Alfonso spinning through the air.

'I've got a record-breaking attempt planned for a week's time at Lookout Point,' he said. 'I've been working up to it for years.'

'You'll manage it!' said Lemmy. 'I know you will.'

Though his legs were wobbly, Alfonso found a way to his feet. He liked a grand gesture as much as he liked telling stories.

'Up there, alone above the clouds,' he said, raising his wings to the ceiling, 'you think you can go on forever. You can spin, duck, fall and stall again and again, wowing crowds and audiences the world over. But, boy, this time my nerve gave out.'

'It sounds to me like all you need is
a good rest,' said Anna.

Alfonso slumped back into the chair.
'I hope so, miss,' he said.

'I know so,' said Anna.

The pigeon flashed her a smile. 'You lot
are too kind,' he said, taking in the lobby
and hotel for the first time. 'Gee whizz,' he
said, 'and I think this hotel is possibly the
most beautiful hotel I ever saw.'

'You're right there,' growled T. Bear.

'Say! Any chance of me taking a room while I recuperate?' asked the pigeon. 'It could be just what I need to get my wings flapping again.'

Lemmy flicked through the bookings diary at the front desk. It was pretty much empty.

'Absolutely, sir,' he said. 'How long will you be staying?'

'Now that's a question,' replied the pigeon. 'How many seeds are there in a birdfeeder?'

'I don't know, sir,' said Lemmy.

'Then let's leave it at that for now,' said Alfonso.

Lemmy handed over a key. 'Room two-one-seven. Second floor. Need any help with your luggage?'

Alfonso turned round to reveal a thin flight bag strapped to his back.

'Flying aerobatics with these wings,' he said with a smile, 'a pigeon has to travel light!'

Alfonso wobbled off towards the lift, testing his wings as he went.

'Looks like we have our first guest of the season,' said Anna with a smile.

2

Some Big Ideas

The arrival of Alfonso Fastbeak highlighted to Anna that the winter season had been too quiet at Hotel Flamingo. There were always fewer guests during the colder months of the year, especially with so many animals in hibernation, but even the restaurant had seen a downturn this year.

With the seasons changing and the

weather warming, Anna decided to do something about it. She set about brainstorming ideas with T. Bear and Lemmy in her office.

'What does the hotel have that no other hotel has?' asked Anna.

'A flamingo lampshade?' said Lemmy.

'We have a lot of those,' agreed T. Bear.

'And flamingo wallpaper,' added Lemmy. 'Not to mention the flamingo bed sheets and dressing gowns.'

'I love my flamingo dressing gown,' said T. Bear.

Anna wished she'd never asked.

'*Apart* from all the flamingos,' she said. 'What do we have that's really, really special? Something that we can sell to guests to get them through our doors.'

'We have a nice ballroom?' suggested Lemmy.

'And we have one of the best chefs in town,' said T. Bear. 'Even if she is scary.'

Anna froze as an idea struck.

'That's it!' she cried, punching the air. Some of Alfonso's words had struck a chord with her. 'We'll prove to the world that she is the greatest chef in town.'

'How?' asked Lemmy.

'We'll have a competition!' she said. 'A Battle of the Chefs!'

'Madame Le Pig throws a mean punch, that's for sure,' said T. Bear, who had experienced the chef's anger first-hand.

'I don't mean like that,' said Anna. 'It can be a feast, and we can sell tickets!'

'It could work,' said T. Bear, thoughtfully.

Anna ran straight out of the door, through the lobby, into the restaurant and banged on the kitchen door.

'What is it?!' squealed Madame Le Pig. 'I am buttering my turnip tarts!'

'I've had an amazing idea,' said Anna, opening the door.

Madame Le Pig stood ready to attack, a buttery brush raised in her trotter. 'Do you not realise how delicate this task is?!' she cried.

'Hear me out,' said Anna, only a little

bit afraid. 'It's been quiet of late round here, hasn't it?'

Madame Le Pig shrugged. 'Yes,' she said. 'I suppose.'

'And you are one of the most brilliant chefs in the world,' said Anna, 'and people should definitely be eating your food.'

The chef looked happy at the way the conversation was heading.

She sniffed. 'I suppose so. Probably the best?'

Anna breathed deeply. 'Then how about a competition between chefs to prove once and for all that you are the best,' said Anna.

'My food would be compared to others?' asked Le Pig.

'I suppose so,' said Anna.

'How?' asked Madame Le Pig. 'My food is incomparable!'

'And that's what we want to show,' said Anna. 'We could sell tickets, and guests could watch and try the food. It would be a fabulous feast!'

'In front of an audience?' said Madame Le Pig. 'No. I do not see any benefit for me.'

'But I see some for the hotel,' said Anna. 'Which would be good for all of us.'

Madame Le Pig snorted and returned to buttering her turnip tarts.

'So what do you think?' asked Anna.

The chef brushed the tarts back and forth in time with her grumpy snorts.

'Who would judge this . . . competition?'

'The guests,' said Anna.

'What do they know?' she grumbled. 'Most creatures do not know their fruit fork from their salad fork.'

Anna certainly didn't know the difference.

'I'll get a proper judge, then,' said Anna. 'I promise.'

'And it will help the hotel?'

'It will do wonders for us,' said Anna.

Madame Le Pig sniffed and banged her trotter on the worktop. 'Then I will do it,' she said. 'Now leave me to my work.'

HOTEL FLAMINGO
BATTLE OF THE CHEFS

Watch Madame Le Pig take on all comers and try out their amazing food in the biggest Battle of the Chefs ever!

Eat and delight in the greatest meals on Animal Boulevard.

Sign up now!
(Special rates for room bookings)

3

The Rivals

Anna spent the rest of the morning creating an advert that would interest every food lover in the land, then sent it off to the local paper. She hadn't been so excited in ages. But now she was left with a problem. Anna needed competition – a Battle of the Chefs without any chefs would be no battle at all.

'There are two that rival Madame Le Pig,' whispered T. Bear. Even though Madame Le Pig was in the kitchen, the last thing he wanted was to enrage her even more, so he kept the volume down. 'The Fat Cat Restaurant is world famous. Peston Crumbletart is more like an artist than a cook!'

'Don't forget Laurence Toot-Toot at the Glitz,' added Lemmy. 'I saw him on TV once. Toot-Toot is unforgettable.'

Anna's face soured. 'The Glitz?'

Owned by a lion called Mr Ruffian, the Glitz was Hotel Flamingo's biggest competitor and a thorn in Anna's side.

'If you want this to be a proper competition,' said T. Bear, 'Toot-Toot's one of the best.'

'How will I get him to come?' asked Anna.

'You'll have to go there and ask,' said T. Bear.

'I don't know about that,' said Anna. The Glitz was the last place she wanted to visit. 'What if I bump into Mr Ruffian?'

'I could come with you,' said T. Bear. 'It's mighty quiet round here right now.'

Anna was already having to fight off her nerves at the prospect of seeing the lion, but she knew she had to be strong.

'OK,' she said. 'If Lemmy can keep charge of the hotel without falling asleep?'

'I wouldn't dream of it,' said Lemmy with a cheeky grin.

'Then let's get going.'

The Fat Cat Restaurant was situated in the bustling heart of the Le Chat Shopping Mall. Anna and T. Bear rang the bell and waited.

'Prepare yourself,' said T. Bear. 'He's won every award going and he's known to be full of himself.'

A giant shadowy shape appeared behind the darkened window. The lock turned and the door opened. Peston

Crumbletart, as big as his reputation, with thick ginger fur, fierce eyes and long twizzly whiskers, stood waiting.

'What?' he said. 'We're shut.'

'Hello,' said Anna. 'I'm here from Hotel Flamingo.'

Peston growled a little. 'That crumbling old hotel on Animal Boulevard?' he said. 'I'm surprised it's not been shut down.'

'That's us,' said Anna. 'Can we come in? I have a proposition for you.'

'I don't let competitors inside,' said the cat.

'I think you'll be interested in this,' said Anna.

Peston twitched his nose and ushered them through with a flick of his paw.

The Fat Cat Restaurant looked every bit the fancy restaurant, with gleaming white tiles on the floor, expensive abstract paintings on every wall and crisp white tablecloths on the tables. Anna was in awe of how clean

and tidy it was. Not even Hilary Hippo could get their hotel this tidy.

'What are you after?' asked Peston, twirling his whiskers.

'We're organising a competition,' said Anna, 'for all the best chefs on Animal Boulevard. We want to find out who is the greatest of all!'

'*I* am the greatest chef on Animal Boulevard,' said Peston. 'There is no competition.'

'Yes. While that may be true,' said Anna, 'Madame Le Pig believes that she is also the best.'

Peston hissed a laugh. 'She's dreaming,' he said.

'But she wants an opportunity to prove it,' said Anna.

'I don't need to prove anything,' said Peston. 'I *am* the best.'

'Wouldn't you like the chance to be crowned the greatest chef on Animal Boulevard in front of an adoring audience?' asked Anna.

Peston scratched his chin. 'Perhaps,' he said. 'I do like winning things.'

Anna held out her hand for Peston to shake. 'Do we have a deal?' she said.

'Yes,' agreed the cat. 'Now go away.'

'I'll send you the details once they're agreed!' said Anna, hurrying out past a shelf of medals and award statues.

'You do that,' growled Peston, starting to clean his ears.

4
Welcome to the Glitz

Anna and T. Bear walked up the long
path over the headland to the Glitz.
Ever since Anna had taken over Hotel
Flamingo, the Glitz's owner Mr Ruffian
had tried to make life unbearable for her.
But with the sound of crashing waves
filling the air, and its stunning views, even
Anna had to admit it stood in the most
wonderful location.

Unfortunately, though, she didn't feel the same about the gigantic white hotel. 'It's not pretty, is it?'

'Nothing compares to Hotel Flamingo, miss,' said T. Bear.

The Glitz's opulent golden doorway and pristine white walls couldn't have been more unwelcoming, and Anna shivered with worry as she stood ready to go in.

A surly bulldog security guard looked them up and down.

'In you go,' he said.

'Right then,' she replied, taking a deep breath.

The polished doors opened out into a gigantic golden lobby that smacked of wealth. Statues of proud lions sat upon

plinths, and thin viaducts sent water flowing around the room, splashing down into pools filled with seaweed, shells and oysters.

Anna walked up to the golden reception desk and tapped the bell. Mr Ruffian surprised her by stepping out from behind a door. She'd thought someone else would have been on the desk. The lion looked like a thundercloud ready to explode.

'Ms Anna Dupont. This is a surprise,' he growled, tapping his huge claws against the desk.

Anna trembled a little, but pulled herself together.

'Mr Ruffian,' she said, 'I would like to speak to your chef, Mr Toot-Toot.'

'Wanting to steal my staff?' he said.

'Heavens, no,' said Anna, trying to smile. 'We are having a competition to crown the greatest chef on Animal Boulevard. I thought Mr Toot-Toot would like to take part.'

'There doesn't need to be a competition,' said Mr Ruffian. 'My chef is clearly the greatest there is.'

'That's not what Peston Crumbletart thinks,' said Anna.

'That know-it-all is on board?'

'He is,' said Anna.

Mr Ruffian growled and picked up his phone. He held up his paw to Anna.

'Laurence. Come to the front desk,' he muttered.

Anna heard a far-off door slam, and then after a few seconds a little hedgehog in a black chef's outfit paced across the

gigantic lobby followed by the divine smell of crushed spices.

'My pickled black beans are frying,' said Laurence Toot-Toot grumpily. 'What is it?'

'Are you the best chef on Animal Boulevard?' asked Mr Ruffian.

The hedgehog spat at his feet. 'Are Toot-Toot's spines sharp?' he sneered.

'That's what I thought,' said Mr Ruffian. 'Still, Hotel Flamingo is running a competition to prove who is the greatest chef in town.'

'Hotel Flamingo?' said Toot-Toot. 'I wouldn't be seen dead in that dump.'

'Hey!' snarled T. Bear. 'Watch your words.'

Toot-Toot showed no fear.

'Toot-Toot is the best,' he said confidently. 'There is no one better.'

'That's not what Madame Le Pig or Peston Crumbletart thinks,' said Anna.

'Le Pig? Her food does not rival mine. Crumbletart? He shows promise, but that is all.'

'Well, imagine if they're crowned the greatest in town, simply because you didn't turn up,' said Anna.

'Because you were too scared,' added T. Bear.

'Toot–Toot is never scared,' snapped the hedgehog.

Mr Ruffian was starting to see the opportunity in the chef's rivalry.

'I suppose it could be good for the hotel and our restaurant,' he said.

'Exactly,' said Anna.

The hedgehog's spines rippled across his back. 'Fine. Then Toot–Toot will take part,' he said. 'And Toot–Toot shall win.'

With that, the hedgehog spat at his feet and hurried back to his kitchen.

'Miss Dupont,' said Mr Ruffian, 'even though your hotel will come out badly in all this, I must applaud your ideas.'

'I should wait and see who the winner is before saying such a thing,' said Anna. 'But thank you all the same.'

5

Flying No More

Lemmy was idling away his time shuffling
paper and binning dried-out old pens
at the front desk when Alfonso Fastbeak
walked into the lobby. He stretched his
legs and stretched his wings, and though
he looked the part he seemed but a mere
shadow of himself.

'Oh, no, no, no!' he muttered.

'Sir?' asked Lemmy.

'Gee whizz, I think I've lost it,' said Alfonso.

'Lost what?'

'My wings don't lift me up any more,' he replied. 'Watch.'

Alfonso flapped as hard as he could, but he barely left the carpet.

'Is there anything I can do to help?' said Lemmy.

'How good are you at flying?' asked Alfonso.

Lemmy rushed from the desk and consoled the pigeon. He showed him to a chair. 'Take a seat,' he said. 'I'll get you a cocoa. That'll cure anything.'

Alfonso took out his poster and gazed wistfully at the photo of him in flight.

'Say, what good's a pigeon without

wings?' he said. 'I may as well go hang out at the fountains and bother tourists for scraps.'

'No!' said Lemmy, returning with a steaming cup of cocoa. 'Don't talk like that. I think you're brilliant.'

'I *was*,' said Alfonso. 'I was the best stunt pigeon this side of the ocean, and I was supposed to be breaking records in just a few days' time, but look at me now!'

The revolving doors spun and Anna arrived back at Hotel Flamingo. She could barely contain her excitement, but upon seeing Alfonso looking so sad she knew something was wrong.

'Lemmy?' she asked.

'Alfonso is in a bad way,' Lemmy replied.

'I'm shot through,' said Alfonso, his head in his wing. 'This stunt pigeon's wings have been clipped.'

'He's forgotten how to fly, miss,' said Lemmy. He cupped his mouth to speak secretly. 'I think he's just lost his confidence after the fall.'

'That's awful,' said Anna. 'There must be something we can do?'

Lemmy shrugged. 'What, though, miss?'

'I have an idea,' she said.

'You do?' said Alfonso.

Anna patted the pigeon on the shoulder. 'I know just the person to call,' she said. 'But first I must speak to our chef.'

•

'We've got a competition!' said Anna excitedly.

Madame Le Pig took hold of a huge chopping knife and readied a huge pumpkin.

'Who is taking part?' she asked.

'Peston Crumbletart,' said Anna.

Madame Le Pig looked unimpressed and gave a dry snort. Unusually, thought Anna, maybe she even looked a bit worried.

'AND Laurence Toot-Toot!' said Anna.

'The three greatest chefs head-to-head at Hotel Flamingo. It is going to be the most amazing event.'

Madame Le Pig cut the pumpkin in half with one almighty chop.

'Good. I am pleased for you,' she said.

'Shall I build a stage?' asked Anna. 'We can have you all working in a line. Lights? Music? Make it a big show?'

Madame Le Pig took another violent chop at the pumpkin.

'These are all unnecessary garnish,' said Madame Le Pig.

'I need nothing more than ingredients and heat.'

'OK,' said Anna. 'But this is a once-in-a-lifetime event. It has to be exciting.'

'That is your problem, not mine,' said the chef, scooping out pumpkin seeds and flicking them angrily to the worktop.

Anna knew when to leave.

'You know best,' she said.

'Yes I do,' said Madame Le Pig. 'I must create a whole new menu. Now go.'

6

Plans are Afoot

Lemmy had done little but answer phone calls all morning. News had spread around Animal Boulevard faster than a rising cake, and the competition was the only thing people were talking about.

'We've already sold out!' said Lemmy as Anna left her office with a huge piece of paper in hand. She'd drawn out the whole plan for the stage and kitchens and needed to give it to Stella. The giraffe was going to have her work cut out.

'SOLD OUT?!' said Anna. 'I don't believe it.'

'Yup!' He laughed. 'The animals around here certainly like their food.'

Anna bathed for a few seconds in the glory of success. And then the reality of it hit. The event had to be amazing and time was running out.

'We've got to get to work,' she said. 'Come next Friday the ballroom has to be fully ready for the showdown to end all showdowns. The Battle of the Chefs!'

'We'll manage it, miss!' said Lemmy.

'Did you find a judge?' asked T. Bear, who'd been listening in while tending to plants in the foyer. 'I mean, I'd happily do it myself, but the other chefs might think I was biased.'

Anna slapped her forehead. 'I've completely forgotten to do that,' she said.

'Want to leave it with me, miss?' asked T. Bear. 'I have a few ideas.'

'Would you?' said Anna.

T. Bear saluted. 'It would be an honour,' he said.

•

The last of the snow had melted, and the sun was shining again on Animal Boulevard. Out on the terrace, clusters of yellow, purple and white flowers had broken through the earth in the flower

beds, and everything was coming back
to life.

Anna danced across the terraces,
brimming with excitement. She found

Stella Giraffe, the hotel's handywoman, hard at work unwrapping protective winter coats from the palm trees.

'STELLA!' she cried. 'I need you!'

Stella knew exactly what was to follow – Anna always wanted something building, and it was never easy. Still, Stella liked a challenge.

'What is it this time?' she asked.

Anna opened up her paper plans, revealing the stage design.

'It's a giant kitchen,' said Anna. 'Actually, it's three kitchens rolled into one.'

'Three kitchens? Three ovens? Three hobs?' said Stella. 'And how long do I have to build it?'

Anna bit her lip. 'A week?'

'Where am I going to find three ovens in a week?' said Stella, waving her hoof in the air like a sword.

'You'll do it! I know you will!' said Anna with a smile.

She walked back past Jojo the otter, who was testing the water in the pool. After being closed throughout winter, the otter was all smiles at the prospect of swimming once more.

'Just perfect,' she said, and leapt in.

Anna was overjoyed to feel the hotel coming alive again.

•

'Where is he, darling?' announced Ms Fragranti, bursting through the door in a flurry of bright pink feathers.

Ms Fragranti was the founder of a stage school for pink flamingos, and she always came to Anna's aid when she needed help. She swept elegantly through the lobby.

'You're here!' said Anna, rushing to give her friend a hug.

Ms Fragranti placed her luggage on the floor and tidied up her scarf.

'When you call, I always answer!' she said.

'Follow me,' said Anna. 'Alfonso is in a bad way.'

'I'll have him dancing the tango in no time,' said Ms Fragranti.

'You do know he wants to fly again?' said Anna, asking for reassurance. 'Not dance.'

'Yes, darling!' said Ms Fragranti. 'But we must take small steps in the gloom before we leap into the dark, yes?'

Anna loved having Ms Fragranti to stay. She always made a difference. They found Alfonso in the Piano Lounge making imaginary aerobatic moves with

his wingtips. He was looking very sorry for himself.

'Alfonso,' said Anna, 'I've got someone here who can help you.'

The pigeon leapt to his feet at the magnificent sight of Ms Fragranti.

'Alfonso Fastbeak, ma'am!' he announced with a salute. 'Fastest pigeon this side of the ocean.'

'How wonderful to meet you, darling,' said Ms Fragranti. 'I hear you are having some difficulties.'

'Gee whizz, that's one way of putting it,' he said. 'What's a bird without flight?'

'Rather useless, I should imagine,' said Ms Fragranti, flapping her gigantic pink wings. 'But we shall have you back in the air in no time. However, we will need a room to workshop our strategy.'

'Already dealt with,' said Anna. 'The Royal Suite is available. How does that sound?'

'That sounds divine,' said Ms Fragranti. 'And the pool is heated still?'

'Exactly as you like it,' said Anna.

The flamingo dipped her neck. 'Terrific,' she said. 'We'll start first thing in the morning!'

7

Testing Flight

After breakfast, Lemmy showed Alfonso to the Royal Suite up on the highest floor in the hotel. He rang the bell and Ms Fragranti opened the door.

'Come on in, darling,' she said. 'Are you staying, Mr Lemmy?'

'Please do,' said Alfonso. 'I'd like the support.'

Lemmy took a seat by the windows

and gazed out over
Animal Boulevard.
It seemed so high up
to him. He gulped,
and turned back
to the room, which
had been cleared of
furniture ready for
the day.

Ms Fragranti
started with some
vocal exercises.

'From the chest!
La, la, la, la!' she
sang, and asked
Alfonso to follow.

'La, la, la, la!'
he tweeted.

'And you, Mr Lemmy!' said Ms Fragranti.

'I'm really not a singer,' said Lemmy.

Ms Fragranti shook her head and very long neck. 'If you are sitting here, you are taking part,' she said.

'La, la, la,' he sang, and flushed red with embarrassment.

'Wonderful, darling,' said Ms Fragranti. 'Do you see? Everyone can sing. Now let us try singing and moving at the same time.'

Ms Fragranti started walking in

circles about the room, and willed Lemmy and Alfonso to follow.

'Do you hear the wind blow?' she sang in her terrific warbling voice.

Lemmy and Alfonso repeated her line for line, and followed her about the room.

'Do you hear the wind blow?'

'*Do you hear the wind blow?*'

Ms Fragranti started flapping her wings, bouncing gently across the floor.

'Let your wings open wide!'

'*Let your wings open wide!*'

Alfonso flapped his wings, but while Lemmy thought he should point out that he didn't have wings, he knew it was a waste of time. He flapped his arms instead.

'Do you see the ground below?'

'*Do you see the ground below?*'

Ms Fragranti was now taking longer leaps around the room, almost to the point of flying.

'Take a leap, start to glide!'

'*Take a leap, start to glide!*'

Lemmy was feeling incredibly silly, but Alfonso was definitely getting closer to flight. They circled round and round and suddenly Ms Fragranti called out, 'FLY, LITTLE BIRD! FLY!'

Alfonso was caught up in the moment – so much so, that he almost did fly. He hovered for a few seconds but then came crashing down and rolled into a wall with a thud.

Ms Fragranti put her wings on her hips. 'Darling,' she said, 'you were so close. I see lots of promise.'

Alfonso rubbed his dizzy head. 'I see lots of stars,' he said.

Ms Fragranti paced the room again. 'It's at times like this we must turn to ballet,' she said, gracefully spinning a pirouette.

'It's not my thing,' said Alfonso, 'but if you think it'll help?'

Lemmy decided it was time to leave.

'I think you'd better focus on Alfonso,' he said. 'I'm just getting in the way here, and I have guests arriving soon.'

'As you wish,' said Ms Fragranti as

Lemmy slipped out through the door. 'Dear pigeon, what do you know of the pas de deux?'

'Pas de what?' said Alfonso.

'A dance of two,' said Ms Fragranti. 'You see, I propose we work on a lift that will mimic flight and take your thoughts away from your wings.'

And for the next two hours Alfonso Fastbeak was tossed, spun and thrown through the air like a white swan in a whirlwind.

A Grass Act

When the first busload of guests arrived, real excitement was felt around the hotel. All the talk was of food and which chef would win. Amid a crowd of animals, two cumbersome Highland cattle, with gigantic horns, blustered up to the front desk.

'Welcome to Hotel Flamingo!' said Lemmy. 'Can I help?'

'It's Mrs Horntop,' said one, who

talked at speed and with urgency. 'We've got a room booked. Here for the competition, of course, though we're keen to try out the regional grasses, aren't we, Norman?'

'Aye. That's right, Petal,' said the other, drawing alongside, holding a guidebook in his hoof. 'Says in here there's at least two hundred.'

'I suppose we must have a few,' said Lemmy, whose knowledge of grass was not as good as it might have been. 'I'll just check the booking.'

'We're expecting to find some good tufts,' continued Mrs Horntop. 'It's so underrated, isn't it, grass?'

'Aye, that's right, Petal,' said Norman.

'Though if everyone ate it, there'd be none left for us, would there?' said Mrs Horntop.

Lemmy smiled and continued to search for their booking as T. Bear struggled through the lobby, lost beneath towers of cases and bags. All Lemmy could see were his paws shuffling along.

'Which rooms?' pleaded T. Bear, wobbling under the weight of the luggage.

Lemmy thought on his feet and found two of the closest empty bedrooms on the first floor. He passed the keys to Mrs Horntop.

'Rooms one-five-four and one-five-five,' he said.

'Thank you!' said T. Bear. And he fell into the lift, narrowly missing Squeak the mouse, who was always ready to deliver guests to their rooms.

'We've heard wonderful things about this hotel,' said Mrs Horntop. 'Excellent

facilities. Wonderful service. Oh, we're very excited –'

There was a strange little tap at the revolving door and Lemmy noticed an odd creature trying to get in.

'Sorry to be rude,' said Lemmy with relief, 'but I must go and help that guest.'

'Aye, you do that. Can't keep a customer waiting!' said Mrs Horntop. 'Very friendly staff here, aren't they, Norman? The reviews did say that, didn't they?'

Lemmy hurried away and opened the revolving door.

'Ah, thank you, kind sir!' said a flamboyant coconut octopus, wearing a magnificent cavalier hat. The octopus was sitting inside a decorated coconut shell full of water, and he dragged himself inside the hotel. 'I find these doors terrifically tricky. Perhaps if I grew some more tentacles I might manage better!' He guffawed loudly.

'Simon Suckerlot?' asked Lemmy.

A slimy tentacle twisted out of the coconut shell to shake Lemmy's paw. Lemmy obliged.

'Sir, you have guessed my name right first time!' quipped the octopus. 'You must be a mind reader!'

Lemmy had guessed it correctly as it was the only octopus in the booking diary. But he decided to play along.

'It is a skill of mine,' he said, sneakily wiping off the slime from his paw.

'Then I feel a game is afoot!' declared Simon. 'Why am I visiting your esteemed hotel, fine sir?'

Lemmy thought long and hard. 'For the Battle of the Chefs?' he asked.

'You truly are a marvel,' said Simon, laughing heartily.

Lemmy walked to the front desk.

'Wonderful,' said Simon. 'And what a gorgeous hotel this is! I can't believe I've not visited before.'

Lemmy handed over a room key. 'Thank you, sir! Any bags?'

'I'm sure you know,' said Simon playfully.

Lemmy could see that all the octopus needed was his shell.

'None, sir!' said Lemmy.

The octopus tapped his forehead with a tentacle. 'How do you do it?!' he said with a chuckle, and dragged himself off to the lift.

A Salty Problem

Stella was beaming with joy outside the hotel.

'Just look at that!' she said proudly, pointing to a line of battered old ovens that had seen better days. 'It's amazing what people throw out these days.'

Hilary and Anna were looking, and were unconvinced.

'Where did you get them from?' asked Anna.

'Two were in a skip, and one on the side of the road,' said Stella.

Hilary opened one of the oven doors and the handle fell off in her hand.

'You expect me to clean up those old rustbuckets?' said Hilary.

'It just needs a bit of elbow grease, that's all,' said Stella. 'We'll soon have them shining.'

'They wouldn't shine even if they were sat on the sun,' said Hilary. 'I do sort of agree with Hilary,' said Anna, scratching at the rusty hobs.

'But finding these saved us a small fortune,' said Stella.

Anna squeezed the broken handle back into place.

'Then I love them!' she said. 'Let's get them inside.'

Hilary rolled her eyes. 'But how are we going to clean them?' she asked. 'I already have the ballroom to clean up, the new worktops to dust . . .'

The list could have gone on, but Anna stopped her.

'I'll help,' she said, understanding that all good managers help out when the going gets tough.

'You bet you will,' said Hilary.

With T. Bear's help they carried the ovens into the lobby, where a group of goats were wanting to check in.

'Can I help?' asked Anna, struggling to hold up her side of the oven.

'Rosie Goat and – MEH! – Sorrel,' said one of the goats. 'We're – MEH! – here for the chef showdown.'

'Lovely,' said Anna, a bead of sweat trickling down her forehead. 'If you just head over to Lemmy at the front desk . . .'

But Lemmy was deep in his own problems.

'Kind sir!' said Simon Suckerlot, scrambling up on to the front desk using his tentacles. Trails of water dripped down behind him. 'I may be having a minor emergency.'

'You are?' said Lemmy, worried.

'Let me ask you,' said Simon, 'does seawater run through the taps here?'

Lemmy had never even considered it.

'I . . .' he said, pausing to think.

'You see,' said Simon, 'a cephalopod such as myself needs a constant source of brine. Not brackish water, you hear – no

mere puddle with a dash of salt – no! I
need proper, solid, stand-you-up-straight
water from the briny deep.'

'I can't say sorry enough!' said Lemmy.

'If I was a sea creature such as a lonely
penguin, who can live in fresh water,
it wouldn't be a problem,' said Simon,
turning all theatrical. He placed his
tentacles on his heart. 'But . . . sadly . . .
I am just an octopus!'

'Sir,' said Lemmy apologetically, 'I shall
sort it out right away.'

The octopus doffed his hat, and slipped
back down to his coconut.

'You are a wonder of the natural
world,' said Simon, rolling away.

10
Bathtime Blues

Lemmy knocked hesitantly on the kitchen door, but there was no reply. He peered through the window to find the room empty.

Eva walked past, carrying a tray of berry smoothies for Sorrel and Rosie Goat.

'Is chef about?' he asked.

'She's buying ingredients,' said Eva cheerfully. 'Apparently there's some special herb she's after.'

'Oh,' said Lemmy.

'Shall I tell her you came by?' she asked.

'NO!' snapped Lemmy. 'Absolutely not.'

Eva shrugged and carried on her business. She seemed to be the only one who wasn't scared of Madame Le Pig.

Lemmy opened the door and sneaked into the kitchen. He searched the cupboards from top to bottom until he found the chef's salt store. There were boxes of smoked salt, pink salt, seaweed salt, as well as a huge bag of the finest sea salt.

'That's the stuff!' he cheered, slinging the sea salt under his arm.

He headed upstairs to Simon Suckerlot's room. The octopus was

lounging at a table reading a collection
of poetry by Sylvia Platypus.

'Hello, sir!' said Lemmy. 'Salt?'

'Wonderful!' said Simon, crawling over
with his shell. 'The bath is full and ready.'

Lemmy slit open the bag of salt,
scooped out a handful and threw it in.

'There you go,' he said.

Simon rolled a tentacle, urging more.

'Keep it coming!' he said.

Lemmy tipped in another handful.

Simon wanted more.

Eventually Lemmy poured in the whole bag. Simon dipped the end of a tentacle into the water and tasted it.

'Too mild,' he said. 'You'd add more seasoning to a plate of fries.'

'Wait here!' said Lemmy.

He raced back down to the kitchen and grabbed all the other salts from the cupboard, sliding herbs and spices into their places to make it look like nothing had been moved. When Lemmy returned, Simon was fully submerged and blowing inky bubbles to the surface.

'Salt, sir!' said Lemmy.

Simon wrapped his tentacles round the taps and pulled himself up.

'Marvellous,' he said. 'Now pour it all in!'

Lemmy did exactly that, and Simon slipped back into the water with a plop.

'MWAH!' said Simon, smacking his beak with his tentacles. 'Now that is perfect. I shall sleep like the king of the sea now!'

And as Lemmy walked away he hoped, above all else, that Madame Le Pig wouldn't notice what had gone missing.

A Cowpat on the Back

Alfonso Fastbeak stumbled out into the lobby from the lift, looking exhausted. Ms Fragranti had worked him to the bone.

'Any luck?' asked Anna, who was pinning posters to the walls.

'Sadly not. I still can't fly, ma'am,' he said. 'Though on the bright side, I'm now excellent at ballet.'

He stopped suddenly with a look of horror on his face.

'Are you all right?' asked Anna.

He slowly raised his leg into the air and brown sludge dripped from his foot. 'How hard is it to use the facilities?!'

'What's that?' asked Anna.

'I'm no expert, miss, but it looks like a cowpat,' said Alfonso.

Anna knelt down and sniffed the circular brown mound.

'It smells like it too,' she said. 'I'll get you a cloth.'

Alfonso attempted to flick the poo from his foot.

'I've landed in worse,' he said. 'It just came as a surprise, that's all.'

At that point the Horntops entered the lobby, chatting happily about food.

'Norman, wasn't that buffalo grass a delight?' said Mrs Horntop.

'Aye. It was delicious!' said Norman.

The Horntops were the only two cows in the hotel, and Anna realised she'd have to confront them. But how do you confront someone about the fact they'd left a cowpat on the floor? she wondered. Direct and to the point, she decided.

'Ah,' said Anna, 'Mrs Horntop, might I have a word?'

'The lunch was wonderful,' said Mrs Horntop, smiling. 'As good as we'd hoped! And we're now heading up to the Barnyard Deli for a grass platter. Isn't that right, Norman?'

'Aye, that's right, Petal,' said Norman.

'I'm pleased you're enjoying yourself,' said Anna. 'However, we have a slight issue.'

'Go on,' said Mrs Horntop.

'There's a cowpat on the floor,' said Anna, direct and to the point.

'Hang my hairy horns,' said Mrs Horntop. 'So there is! Who would have done such a thing? Norman, have you seen that mess on the floor over there? Awful, isn't it?'

'Aye,' he replied. 'Terrible. Some cows have no manners.'

'No manners at all,' said Mrs Horntop. 'Now, we must get

going so we don't miss our reservation.'

'Aye, that's right, Petal,' said Norman, checking his watch. 'That grass has to be freshly cut, or it loses its colour.'

'So it wasn't one of you?' asked Anna.

Mrs Horntop flushed red with embarrassment. 'Us?' she said. 'Never. My Norman is very well trained. As am I.'

'Aye, Petal, that's right,' he replied. 'Come on, love.'

Anna was left stunned.

'I bet it's all that grass they eat,' said Alfonso, shaking his head. 'They just don't have any control.'

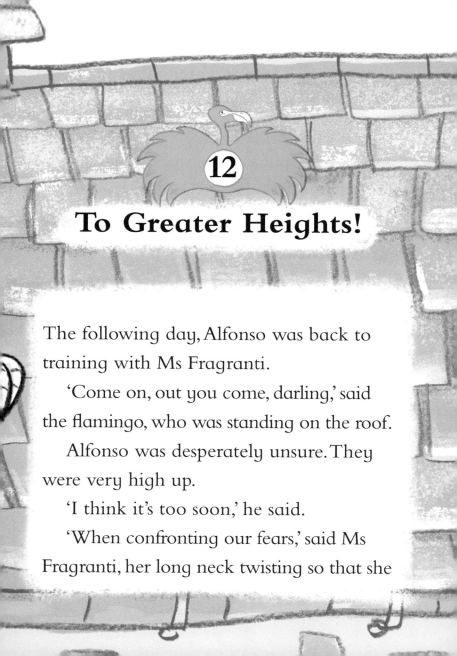

12

To Greater Heights!

The following day, Alfonso was back to training with Ms Fragranti.

'Come on, out you come, darling,' said the flamingo, who was standing on the roof.

Alfonso was desperately unsure. They were very high up.

'I think it's too soon,' he said.

'When confronting our fears,' said Ms Fragranti, her long neck twisting so that she could see him, 'we are confronting life itself. If we don't move forward, then backwards is the only other direction available.'

'What about staying right where we are?' he said. 'That's another option.'

Ms Fragranti reached her wing through the Royal Suite window and Alfonso took hold.

'If you're sure,' he said.

'Alfonso Fastbeak!' said Ms Fragranti with such confidence and energy that she could have roused a snail into flight. 'You are a death-defying, loop-the-looping stunt pigeon. All I ask is that you sit up here and feel the wind in your feathers. Breathe it in, darling.'

Alfonso did as he was asked and clambered out on to the roof.

'My legs don't want to move,' he said, sitting down as fast as he could. Gravity weighed very heavy on him, pushing him flat against the tiles.

'It is better than yesterday,' Ms Fragranti said, and stretched her wings. 'Look at you! You may not be flying, but you are up high, as a bird like you should be.'

Alfonso breathed deeply and let the smell of fresh sea air fill his lungs. It was true: he did feel a tingle of excitement in his cheeks. The old Alfonso was returning.

'Try standing up,' said Ms Fragranti.

'I don't know if I can,' said Alfonso.

The flamingo willed him on. 'I am here to help you,' she said, tapping him on the chest. 'Confidence is found in here.'

Alfonso cooed, puffed up his feathers and stood up.

'Wonderful, darling!' said Ms Fragranti. 'How does it feel?'

'Say, I reckon that it's getting a little

bit better,' he said, loosening up.

But at that very moment his claws lost their grip. He skidded downwards, never quite regaining his hold. Ms Fragranti

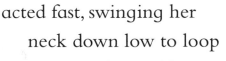 acted fast, swinging her neck down low to loop round him. Alfonso gripped her scarf and finally stopped sliding.

'Gee whizz, can we go back inside now?' he asked.

'I think so, darling, yes,' agreed Ms Fragranti.

They rested for a moment in the Royal Suite, before Alfonso decided he'd had enough.

'Aww, shucks, I can't do it,' he said. 'I feel like fear is eating me from the inside.'

Ms Fragranti tipped her beak and looked kindly upon him.

'We all suffer from stage fright at some

point in our lives, darling,' she said. 'Yet we mustn't let it rule us.'

'Thank you, ma'am,' said Alfonso, 'but I think it's ruling me.'

Alfonso headed downstairs and took some less terrifying air out on the terrace.

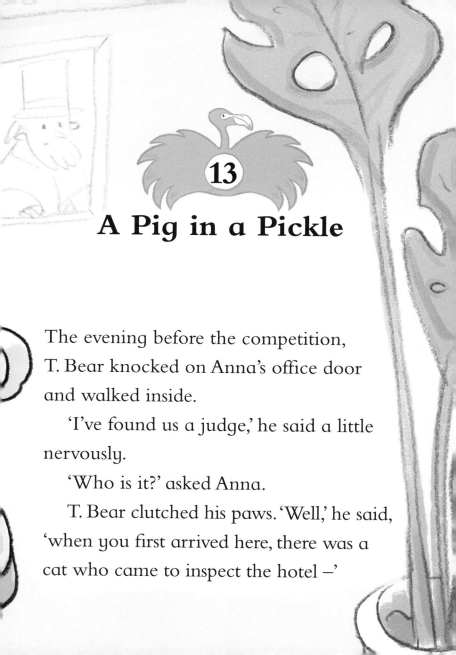

13

A Pig in a Pickle

The evening before the competition,
T. Bear knocked on Anna's office door
and walked inside.

'I've found us a judge,' he said a little
nervously.

'Who is it?' asked Anna.

T. Bear clutched his paws. 'Well,' he said,
'when you first arrived here, there was a
cat who came to inspect the hotel –'

'Mr Grayson?' said Anna.

'That's right,' replied T. Bear. 'He was very official, and fair, and I thought he might be a good fit.'

'That's a brilliant idea,' said Anna. 'And he liked us as well. I'd better tell Madame Le Pig.'

Anna rushed to the kitchen. The restaurant was filled with guests, but the chef was unusually quiet.

'What is it?' said Madame Le Pig, finishing off a round of desserts.

'We have a judge,' said Anna. 'Mr Grayson, the hotel inspector!'

'What does it matter to me?' said Le Pig with a shrug. 'I have my new menu. That is all I need.'

'But we know he likes your food,' said Anna. 'The other chefs won't stand a chance.'

Madame Le Pig placed the puddings at the service hatch and dinged a bell for Eva. She huffed. 'I hope you are right,' she said.

Anna was stopped dead by the chef's words. This did not sound like the Madame Le Pig she knew.

'You hope?' said Anna. 'I know you will win.'

'HOW CAN YOU?' snapped the chef, who became instantly flushed with rage. 'I have spent the past fifteen years fighting to be the best chef in the world. It is not easy being brilliant!'

'I know it's not,' said Anna.

For the first time she realised that Madame Le Pig was worried about losing the competition. And what would happen if she did lose? It didn't bear thinking about.

Madame Le Pig sniffed. 'I have to work,' she said.

'Sorry, yes,' said Anna, and she left the kitchen, feeling terrible.

Luckily Ms Fragranti was waiting for Anna in the lobby as she returned to her office.

'A word, darling?' said the flamingo.

'Yes?' said Anna with a sigh. 'More problems?'

They walked into the office and Anna sat down.

'I don't think I can help him,' said Ms  Fragranti. 'Alfonso needs more than a coach; he needs . . .' Ms Fragranti was unusually lost for words. 'He needs to find himself. Only once he believes in himself will he soar again across the sky.'

'I see,' said Anna.

'And you, darling, you're not your usual self?' asked Ms Fragranti.

'I think I've forced Madame Le Pig into a situation she didn't want to be in,' said Anna.

'This competition?'

Anna nodded.

Ms Fragranti spread a wing round Anna's shoulder to comfort her. 'It is a hard lesson to learn, but prizes are not everything, darling,' said the flamingo. 'Madame Le Pig's brilliance is found in her food, not the trophies on her shelf.'

'I thought she'd just get angry and shout a lot, like always,' said Anna. 'I didn't think she'd start to worry about losing.'

'Winning is lovely,' said Ms Fragranti, 'but losing? Now that can affect us all.'

'I see that now,' said Anna, growing more and more desperate. 'All the chefs are amazing. Oh, how do I make sure she wins?'

'You don't,' said Ms Fragranti, horrified. 'Cooking is like art – it is not a game. It cannot be won, and you cannot cheat.'

'But what if she loses?' asked Anna. 'It will ruin her.'

'You must believe in her no matter what,' said Ms Fragranti.

Anna's head fell to the desk. 'Will you stay for tomorrow?' she asked. 'I like having you here.'

'Of course, darling,' said Ms Fragranti. 'I would never leave in your hour of need! I can keep an eye on your chef. She doesn't scare me.'

'Thank you,' said Anna. 'Now I'd better go and check how the ballroom is coming along.'

14
Cow Confidential

With just hours to go before the competition the hotel was filled with guests. There was an exciting buzz about the place and it wasn't because of the party of bees that had come to stay.

Anna headed down through the lobby staircase to the ballroom. Giant photographs of the three chefs hung on the walls, and Stella was wrestling with some disagreeable copper pipes. With Hilary's help she'd worked day and night to create the makeshift kitchens, and now they were looking exactly how Anna had designed them.

'It's perfect!' she said.

Upon the stage there were three cooking stations in place, each with a fridge, an oven and hob, and a bench for preparing food. Stella was deep in thought, plumbing in the gas pipes. She tightened a bolt, then stood up and nodded happily.

'It's all or nothing!' said Stella, and she flicked a switch. A crown of flames burst out of a hob. 'And we're cooking on gas!'

'I'll get T. Bear to sort out the chairs and tables,' said Anna. 'And then I think we're almost ready.'

'And can I have a sleep?' asked Stella.

'Absolutely,' said Anna.

She marched back upstairs full of excitement, only to find another cowpat lying in front of the reception desk.

'Lemmy?' she said, jolting the lemur into life. 'Did you see who did this?'

Lemmy peered over the desk. 'It wasn't me,' he said.

'I know it wasn't you,' said Anna.

'I'll call Hilary,' said Lemmy.
'She won't like it.'

'I don't like it either!' said Anna. 'I'm going to have to say something to the cows. You can't just go around doing things like this on other people's carpets!'

'You tell 'em, miss!' said Lemmy.

'I just have to find the right moment,' said Anna, 'but they can't be doing this at the food competition. That would be awful!'

'And get us shut down!' said Lemmy.

Anna's face turned to horror. The one

person with the power to shut down her hotel was the one person judging the Battle of the Chefs: Mr Grayson, the world's most difficult hotel inspector. She had to tell the cows immediately.

•

Anna found the Horntops out on the terrace, lounging by the pool. With all their fur they couldn't notice the slight chill in the air.

'Mrs Horntop?' said Anna.

'Aye,' said the cow, who was tucking into a rolled-up mini bale of hay. 'What can I do for you?'

'It's the cowpats,' said Anna. 'I've just found another!'

'Oh no, it's nothing to do with us, is it, Norman?'

'Aye, Petal,' said Norman, chewing on a pack of grass crisps. 'That's right.'

'The thing is,' said Anna, 'we have to find a way to stop them – oh gosh, how do I say this? – appearing? I'll have to ask you to leave if it continues.'

'Us?' said Mrs Horntop. 'Leave?'

'There's a hotel inspector visiting tonight,' said Anna. 'He can shut us down if there are . . . well, you know. If those things are all over the floor.'

'Shut you down?' said Norman. 'But it's nothing to do with us, is it, Petal?'

Mrs Horntop pulled Anna to one side and whispered into her ear. 'I don't want him knowing,' she said.

'Knowing what?' asked Anna.

'I'm grass-intolerant,' said Mrs Horntop.

'But it's his favourite thing. Eating grass is what he loves more than anything, and, well, it goes right through me.'

'But he loves you, doesn't he?' asked Anna. 'He'd understand if you told him.'

'Well, I suppose I could try,' said Mrs Horntop thoughtfully. 'Perhaps he would!'

'Then for the good of all of us I think it's best you tell him,' said Anna. 'And stop eating grass.'

'Do you think?' asked Mrs Horntop.

'Yes I do,' said Anna firmly.

15

The Warm-Up

Late in the afternoon, the three competing chefs gathered at Hotel Flamingo. They all carried their own ingredients and kitchen implements, holding them close to their chests.

'Here are the rules,' said Anna. 'You will cook three courses: one starter, one main and one pudding. The judge's decision is final.'

'Who is the judge?' asked Peston Crumbletart, the huge cat chef.

'His name is Mr Grayson,' said Anna.

The three chefs looked lost for words. Grayson's reputation was fierce.

'I don't think he even likes food!' said Toot-Toot the hedgehog.

Peston Crumbletart twirled his whiskers. 'You sound scared,' he said.

'NO!' said Toot-Toot, spitting on the ground. 'I am not scared.'

Madame Le Pig remained silent, and Anna looked at her nervously, hoping she was all right.

'Mr Grayson is the best there is,' said Anna. 'He will be fair, I know it. Now, if you all want to make your way downstairs, you can get a feel for the kitchens.'

Despite Peston Crumbletart's best attempts at belittling the stage, even he was impressed.

'It's cleaner than I imagined it would be,' he said, arranging his ingredients and pans around the worktop.

'Not a patch on the Glitz,' said Toot-Toot. The hedgehog had a special range of implements branded with his name. He laid them out in size order alongside the oven.

Madame Le Pig shuffled back and forth in a way that was most unlike her.

'Is everything all right for you?' asked Anna.

'There is heat; there are ingredients. I am fine,' she said.

'As long as you are OK,' said Anna.

'I am,' she snorted. 'I do not need special treatment.'

'Then if everyone is happy,' said Anna, 'it's time to leave the stage. The guests will be arriving soon.'

She led the chefs through to a spare room beside the ballroom, and returned to the lobby, where guests had started

to gather. There was a thrilling air of excitement, and lots of talk about what the chefs might be cooking.

Anna found Lemmy at the desk.

'Any more cowpats?' she asked.

'Not that I've found,' he said. 'What did you say to them?'

Anna paused, thinking that no one else needed to know about Mrs Horntop. 'It was just a misunderstanding,' she said. 'They do things quite differently where they're from.'

'Oh, good!' said Lemmy. 'That could have been really awkward.'

'Yes it could,' agreed Anna.

And with that she went and sat in her office and read through her introductions for the competition. There was now a lot more at stake than Anna had bargained for. She drew a deep breath and steeled herself.

16
Return of the Cat

'We meet again,' said the hotel inspector. Dressed in a raincoat and carrying a briefcase, Mr Grayson seemed pleased to be back.

T. Bear shook Mr Grayson's paw. 'Thank you for coming,' he said.

'Who could resist an opportunity to eat food by the three best chefs on Animal Boulevard?' said Mr Grayson.

'Good evening, sir!' said Anna, hurrying over. 'We're all ready, if you'll come through to the ballroom.'

'My pleasure,' said Mr Grayson.

She showed him downstairs. Guests were already at their tables, enjoying the occasion, and there was a real excitement in the air. Anna placed Mr Grayson at his own table alongside the stage and Mr Ruffian, who watched on gleefully. The Horntops were there, chewing away on a packet of grass-free meadow snacks, as were Simon Suckerlot and Sorrel and Rosie Goat. And they were all counting down the minutes to the start.

Alfonso and Ms Fragranti sat together at the back of the room alongside T. Bear. They cheered as Anna took to the stage.

'Welcome to Hotel Flamingo for our Battle of the Chefs!' Anna announced.

The crowd whooped and hollered, and Anna gave T. Bear the nod. He switched on the music, and a loud rock song by The Nocturnal Animals burst out of the speakers.

'Introducing one of the finest chefs of his generation . . .' said Anna, 'PESTON CRUMBLETART!'

The huge cat jogged into the ballroom, swinging his arms around. His apron flapped as he leapt on to the stage and bowed. He took his position at his bench.

'And now,' said Anna, 'fresh from the Glitz . . . Laurence Toot-Toot!'

Toot-Toot strode into the ballroom, dressed in his signature black outfit. He lifted his paws, willing the audience to give him even more applause. They roared louder as he clambered on to the stage and found his bench. He slammed a chopper into the chopping board. Toot-Toot meant business.

'And finally!' said Anna. 'Hot from the kitchens of Hotel Flamingo . . . Madame Le Pig!'

The music boomed louder. The applause became deafening. But Madame Le Pig did not appear.

'Um . . .' said Anna. Her eyes darted across the room, skipping left to right in search of her chef. Her stomach turned over, and a wave of fear and sickness crept through her body. What if Madame Le Pig was having one of her moments?

Anna tried again. 'Let me present . . . Madame Le Pig!'

The door opened with a squeal, and finally Madame Le Pig ventured out. But all was not well and Anna could see it. Despite the roar of the crowd, Le Pig looked unhappy as she trod uneasily across the ballroom.

She stepped up on to the stage, turned briefly to the crowd and all the colour drained from her face. She gulped, clenched her trotters and raced from the ballroom.

'Madame?' said Anna.

The crowd fell silent. Mr Ruffian looked immensely pleased with himself as Anna grew increasingly uncomfortable on stage.

'Leave it to me, darling!' said Ms Fragranti. She danced out of the ballroom, past Alfonso, and found Madame Le Pig nearby, shivering in the corridor.

'What's wrong, my friend?' she asked.

'This!' said Madame Le Pig. 'This is all wrong! I should never have agreed to it.'

'Madame Le Pig,' Ms Fragranti said, 'you are the best chef there is. And that is your crowd. They're here to see you.'

'I know that,' she replied through a grimace. 'But I cannot go on the stage. I CANNOT!'

Ms Fragranti could see she was suffering from stage fright, just like Alfonso.

'I can help you,' she said.

'NO ONE CAN HELP ME!' squealed Le Pig.

Madame Le Pig held up her trotters, which were shaking violently. 'I cannot cook with these things!' she snorted. 'They are only good for whisking eggs!'

'Then whisk eggs, darling,' said Ms Fragranti. 'I know how good you are; you know how good you are. Don't let anything stop other people seeing it.'

'But I always cook alone!' she said. 'Not in front of a million creatures.'

'Just imagine the crowd aren't wearing any clothes,' said Ms Fragranti. 'That's

how I do it.'

    Madame Le Pig's snout screwed up. 'URGH!' she squealed. 'That would be horrible!'

    'WAIT!' said Ms Fragranti. 'Listen.'

    The crowd were chanting 'Le Pig! Le Pig!' over and over.

    'They are your people. They love you,'

said the flamingo. 'Madame Le Pig, you are AMAZING.'

Madame Le Pig took a deep breath and listened to the crowd. Something stirred deep down inside her.

'I am AMAZING,' she said, colour returning to her cheeks.

'You are the best!' said Ms Fragranti.

The chef's trotters stopped shaking. Steam rocketed from her snout.

'I AM THE BEST!' she squealed.

'And are you ready to cook?'

'I AM READY!' cried the pig.

And with that she stomped off into the ballroom. The cheers rang out. Anna's fear-filled face lightened into a smile, and the Battle of the Chefs had begun.

17

For Starters

With an air of solid concentration and intense creativity Madame Le Pig, Peston Crumbletart and Toot-Toot locked horns in combat.

'And to begin,' announced Anna, 'we have the starters!'

She walked across the stage to Madame Le Pig, who had been feverishly chopping, trimming, dipping and broiling.

Sweat dripped from her snout under the glaring lights. With a slam of her trotter she presented her dish.

'Roasted fleas with a tart redcurrant sauce!' announced Madame Le Pig triumphantly.

The crowd clapped as Eva ran across the stage, picked up the plate and delivered it to Mr Grayson.

Anna stepped sideways to Peston Crumbletart, who had been peeling, blanching, baking and grilling with such precision that he looked in complete control. He loaded food on to a plate, then set alight a tiny jug of liquid.

The smell of the sea floated across the ballroom and the crowd went wild.

'Crunchy krill crackers with a spicy chilli dip and seaweed drift!' declared Peston Crumbletart.

Eva Koala returned for the second dish, and Anna moved on to Toot-Toot. He grated, seared, oiled and sizzled with the flourish of a dancer. When the food was ready he spun and leapt into the air.

'Wilted fragrant leaves with a gritty mud dressing!' he cried.

The crowd clapped again, and Eva removed the plate.

The crowd hushed as Mr Grayson tasted and tested each dish. He made notes in a little book. Once finished, he passed the plates back to Eva.

'Would anyone like to try the dishes?' asked Anna.

Everyone in the room cried out for a taste, and Eva did her best to distribute them in tiny taster pots.

While the chefs took a five-minute break, Hilary ran on to the stage and swept the floor before wiping the worktops clean, refreshing them for the second round.

'Do we have a winner for the first round?' asked Anna.

Mr Grayson nodded. He had three cards in front of him, each bearing the photo of a chef. He lifted that of Peston Crumbletart.

'Peston Crumbletart takes the lead!' announced Anna.

Although cheers reverberated around
the room, the crowd were divided.

Mrs Horntop rose from her seat. 'The
fleas should have won,' she stated angrily.
'They were easily the tastiest, weren't
they, Norman?'

'Aye, that's right, Petal,' said Norman.

'Thank you, Mrs Horntop,' said Anna,
calling the chefs back on stage.

Peston strode on, twirling his whiskers. He was loving this.

'And, next up, we have the main courses!' said Anna. 'Are you ready? Then begin!'

The chefs were straight back to the chopping boards, working with speed and authority. This time, Anna approached

Toot–Toot first. He spun a plate on his fingertips before placing it on to the worktop.

'Curried twig sticks with a minty yoghurt dip!' yapped Toot-Toot.

'Remarkable!' said Anna, as Eva picked up the dish and delivered it to Mr Grayson.

Peston Crumbletart stirred a pan with speed, whipping up a bubbling froth before pouring it over the dish.

'Diced carrot and cashew nut roast with a delicate fruit froth!' he said, stepping back triumphantly, his paws raised in celebration.

Eva took the meal to Mr Grayson, and Anna returned to Madame Le Pig. Anna gave her a smile, silently willing her on. With a sizzling red sauce swirled around the plate, Madame Le Pig's meal was complete.

'Battered broccoli and mushroom risotto with a sticky date sauce!' she said, punching her trotter into the air.

Eva took the plate to Mr Grayson, and with all the mains now in front of him he picked up a fork and dug into each one.

'Amazing scenes here,' said Anna into the microphone, as Mr Grayson made notes.

He finally came to a decision, and lowered his paws to the cards. He lifted Toot-Toot's face above his head.

'And Toot-Toot takes the second round!' said Anna, nerves racing through her now like never before.

Anna could see Madame Le Pig was struggling to come to terms with being last. As the chefs went off for another break and Hilary cleaned up, Anna approached her to give her some support.

'Win the dessert round and it's a tie,' she said positively.

'I have planned all the wrong meals!' said Le Pig. 'ACH! I should have cooked what I know.'

'Just cook your favourite dish,' said
Anna. 'The one that everyone knows you
for. The one that everyone loves.'

Madame Le Pig sniffed in agreement.
'I shall try,' she said, finding some resolve.
'NO! I SHALL DO!'

Just Desserts

The final round was under way. Madame Le Pig scrambled through her box for everything she needed for the dessert. But something was missing. She pulled Anna to one side of the stage. The other chefs noticed something was up, but they were against the clock. They couldn't let it bother them.

'Seaweed salt,' said Madame Le Pig. 'Where is it?'

'I don't know what you mean,' said Anna.

'Someone has been in my things! It is missing!' said Le Pig.

'Do you need it?' asked Anna.

'OF COURSE I NEED IT!' blasted Madame Le Pig.

Lemmy raced over from the side of the ballroom. Peston growled as he neared.

'What's wrong?' asked Lemmy.

Anna shielded her mouth. 'Her seaweed salt's gone missing,' she said.

Lemmy's ears drooped, but he knew honesty was always the best policy.

'Oh,' he mumbled. 'That might be my fault.'

'What?' asked Anna.

'I needed it to make the octopus's bathwater salty,' he said.

'You did what?!!' screamed Madame Le Pig. 'That salt is the most expensive on the planet!'

'Simon was really happy,' said Lemmy. 'It was a life-or-death situation.'

'Here,' growled Peston Crumbletart. He slid a bag of salt over on to Madame Le Pig's worktop. 'Your nonsense is breaking my concentration.'

'I cannot use this rubbish!' said
Madame Le Pig. 'It needs to be seaweed
salt!'

Peston shrugged. 'Don't use it then,'
he said. 'See how the judge reacts to badly
seasoned scones.'

Madame Le Pig turned her nose up,
but gripped the salt. 'I have no choice,'
she said angrily.

'I'm sorry,' said Lemmy.

'If it was life or death,' said Le Pig, 'then I cannot argue. Now leave me to cook!'

The chefs cooked on, with the crowd growing rowdier with each passing minute. Peston completed his dish first.

'Erupting chocolate volcano in a mound of frozen berries!' he cried. He tipped a tiny spoonful of powder into the dish, and chocolate oozed upwards. The crowd couldn't cope with such magic. Mrs Horntop passed out at its brilliance.

Eva carried it to Mr Grayson, splurts of chocolate landing on her nose. She happily licked them off.

Next up was Toot-Toot. With a plate laid out ready, he threw a pear into the air and, as it fell, chopped it into ridiculously thin slices. They landed perfectly aligned on the plate.

'Crunchy cinnamon biscuit, dipped in crackling sherbet with a sweet pear topping!' he announced.

The crowd loved that one even more than the chocolate volcano. The plate was carried off to Mr Grayson, and Anna stepped across to the final dessert, that of Madame Le Pig's.

She carefully positioned a plateful of cakes on to a tray, and added a pot of jam next to it. There was no showing off needed.

'And our final dish of the battle,' said Anna.

'My famous squid scones with seaweed jam,' said Madame Le Pig. 'The Queen

Penguin's favourite dish!'

The crowd roared, as though hearing a favourite song come on the radio, and Eva carried the final dish across to Mr Grayson.

The three chefs removed their aprons and placed them on the worktops, and Hilary quickly cleaned the area.

Mr Grayson asked for a moment's silence to deliberate, and the crowd obeyed. He scribbled a few final notes, tasted the food a second time, and put his pen down.

'I have made my decision,' said Mr Grayson. 'Chefs, would you like to come out front?'

The chefs walked to the front of the stage dutifully. Anna passed the judge the

microphone and took a step back.

'Frankly,' said Mr Grayson, without expression, 'I have never tasted better food than I have tonight. But I know you need a winner. So, the winner is . . .'

He waited.

'Hurry up!' snorted Madame Le Pig.

And waited.

And . . .

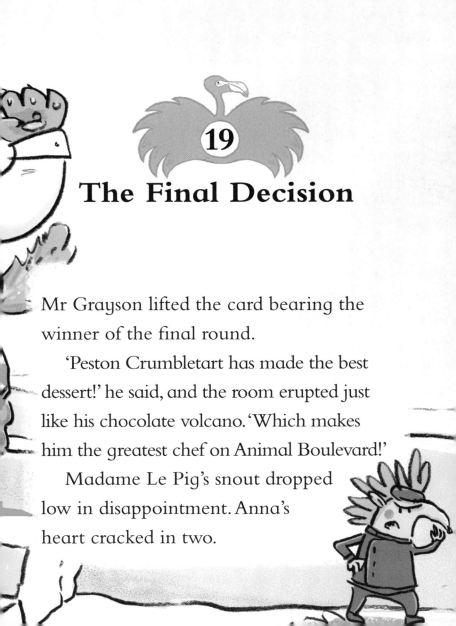

19

The Final Decision

Mr Grayson lifted the card bearing the winner of the final round.

'Peston Crumbletart has made the best dessert!' he said, and the room erupted just like his chocolate volcano. 'Which makes him the greatest chef on Animal Boulevard!'

Madame Le Pig's snout dropped low in disappointment. Anna's heart cracked in two.

Mr Ruffian booed loudly. 'Rubbish!' he roared. 'Toot-Toot is clearly the greatest chef!'

'I disagree,' said Mr Grayson. 'Every chef here is excellent in their own special way. Tonight, however, Peston's dishes were a little more fragrant, a touch sweeter, and a hint more original. And now every guest can come and taste them.'

As the crowd cheered again, Anna put her arm round Madame Le Pig, consoling her. 'I'm so sorry,' she said. 'I think your food is the greatest. We all do here at Hotel Flamingo. And prizes aren't everything. I know that now. This whole competition has been good for the hotel, but not for you.'

'ACH!' said Le Pig, coming to terms with the loss. 'Sometimes it is good to be challenged. Without fear there can be no joy. I know my food is the best, and that is all I need.'

Anna threw both arms round Madame Le Pig, and squeezed her so tight her hat fell off.

'ENOUGH!' squealed Le Pig, swatting her off with her trotters. 'GET AWAY!'

Anna squeezed a little bit tighter, before letting go. 'Thank you,' she said.

As the guests swamped the stage and dug into the food, Toot-Toot stropped out of the ballroom, spitting at the floor.

'I am the best!' he declared, throwing his hat into Mr Ruffian's lap before striding from the hotel.

'It's a fix,' growled Mr Ruffian, before he too left the building.

Anna was full of relief that the night had been a success, despite the result. As Madame Le Pig left the ballroom and

returned to the sanctuary of her kitchen, Anna knew that everyone would be talking about the Battle of the Chefs and Hotel Flamingo for a long time to come.

•

Later that night, Alfonso was sitting in the Piano Lounge listening to Ms Fragranti sing a song about a lonely, blue flamingo. Once the ballroom was tidy, Anna and the rest of the staff filed in to celebrate a job well done.

Anna took a seat next to Alfonso, who was looking cheerful.

'It's good to see you with a smile on your face,' said Anna.

'After that who wouldn't?! Gee whizz, what a show,' he replied. 'How Madame Le Pig got straight back up there on stage to do battle . . . Amazing, really. She has real guts.'

'Just like you,' said Anna.

'Oh, I don't know about that any more, ma'am,' said Alfonso. 'Tomorrow, when I leap from Lookout Point, it'll be just me and the wind.'

'That's not true,' said Anna. 'We'll be there.'

'You will?' said Alfonso.

'We all want you to succeed,' she said.

'But only I can do the jump,' he said. 'What if I bottle it again?'

Anna tapped Alfonso on the chest. 'You've got to take us with you, in your heart,' she said.

'You think?' said Alfonso.

'I do,' said Anna.

Alfonso cooed and rolled his shoulders, finding his confidence.

'All right, then,' he said. 'Tomorrow is a new day. I'm going to face my demons.'

'And we'll be there cheering you on,' said Anna. 'You can do it, Alfonso.'

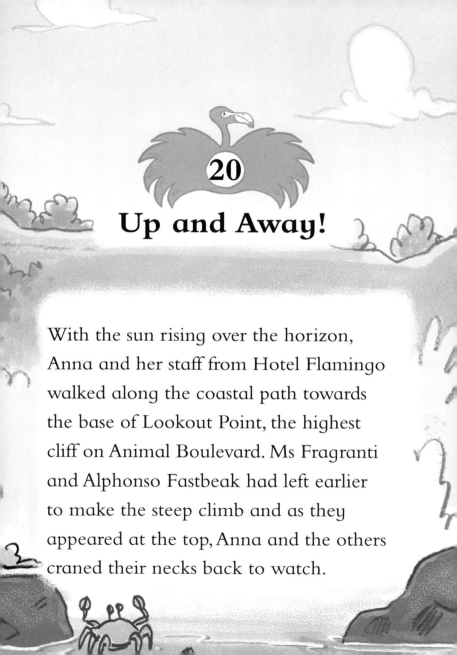

20

Up and Away!

With the sun rising over the horizon, Anna and her staff from Hotel Flamingo walked along the coastal path towards the base of Lookout Point, the highest cliff on Animal Boulevard. Ms Fragranti and Alphonso Fastbeak had left earlier to make the steep climb and as they appeared at the top, Anna and the others craned their necks back to watch.

'They're really high up,' said Lemmy.

'Are you sure this is safe?' asked T. Bear.

'Ach! It's nothing,' said Madame Le Pig, sniffing. 'I have jumped from higher, and I don't have wings.'

At the summit of Lookout Point, Alfonso prepared himself for flight. He zipped up his flight jacket and flipped his goggles down over his eyes.

'Are you ready, darling?' asked Ms Fragranti.

'You bet,' said Alfonso, and he shuffled closer to the cliff edge. The wind was strong. He took a deep breath, filling his lungs with fresh air.

'We believe in you,' said Ms Fragranti. 'But you must also believe in yourself. You *are* a bird and you *can* fly.'

'I'm the best stunt pigeon there has ever been,' he said.

'That's it,' said Ms Fragranti. 'You can do this!'

Alfonso stretched out his wings.

'We're here for you, darling,' added Ms Fragranti.

Back down on the ground, Lemmy crossed every finger and toe on every paw.

'What happens if he crashes again?' he asked.

'He won't,' said Anna.

'I'll catch him if I have to,' said T. Bear.

They saw Alfonso ready himself, now just a grey blur on the clifftop.

'There he goes!' said Anna.

With three big flaps of his wings Alfonso leapt off the ledge. But he didn't rise up. He dropped down.

'Good grief!' said Anna. 'He's not flying; he's falling.'

'Get your arms ready!' cried Lemmy.

T. Bear steadied himself, his teeth clenched, paws outstretched.

Despite everything, Alfonso was smiling as he headed at deadly speed towards the ground. He believed in himself, his wings felt strong, and as soon as he could see the faces of the crowd below, he pulled back. His body soared upwards, and with three flaps of his wings he performed a daring loop-the-loop high above Hotel Flamingo.

Lemmy collapsed into T. Bear's arms.

'He did it!' cheered Anna.

Ms Fragranti soared from the cliff and joined Alfonso in the sky. They performed

a victory lap together, then flew back down to the ground to huge cheers. Alfonso landed with his signature Impossible Twisting Backflip, proving that it was definitely not impossible.

'Congratulations!' said Anna. 'You did it!'

'I told you so,' said Madame Le Pig with a snort.

'Gee whizz, what a ride,' said Alfonso, resting his wings on his knees.

'You made it, darling!' said Ms Fragranti. 'You are back to your best.'

'I really am,' said Alfonso, wiping his brow, 'and it's all thanks to Hotel Flamingo.'

Anna beamed with pride. 'That's what we're here for,' she said, smiling.

A NOTE FROM THE AUTHOR

Writing a story about an animal hotel is a dream come true for me. I love learning about animals (my favourites are lemurs!) and I love drawing them, but I particularly love customer service.

So, as much as I'd like to stay at Hotel Flamingo and eat Madame Le Pig's amazing food, I would actually really like to work there. Yes, you heard right. Tidying the place up, planning and cooking meals, booking shows, making people happy . . . oh, that would be better than anything!

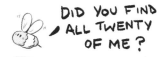

DID YOU FIND ALL TWENTY OF ME?